MONSTER CAKE

by Rebecca Dickinson

SCHOLASTIC INC.

New York Toronto London Auckland Sydney Mexico City New Delhi Hong Kong

Library of Congress Cataloging-in-Publication Data available
ISBN 0-439-06752-9

12 11 10 9 8 7 6 5 4 3 2 1   00 01 02 03 04

Printed in the U.S.A. 24
First printing, September 2000

Rats in the cake,

Bats in the cake,

Lizards in the pan.

Baking a monster birthday cake as quick as we can.

Roll in it,

Stomp on it,

Sprinkle it with bugs.

Spread on thick, green frosting

made from garden slugs.

Powder it with moth dust,

Decorate with fish,

Poke in lots of candles for a birthday wish.

Get our best black tablecloth
made from spiders' silk.

Fill up Mommy's favorite glass

with iguana milk.

FARM FRESH 2% IGUANA MILK

Now run out to the garden and pick
a nice dead flower.

Hurry! Quick!
She'll wake up soon.
We've been up an hour!

Great! Let's see...

Hold on just a minute—!
Oh, for badness sake!

We've got to have more than just monster birthday cake!

Hmmmmm....How about...

Rotten apple yogurt

on earthworm ketchup roast,

garlic-stuffed potato bugs

with a slice of toast?

Pickled armadillos, dandelion stew,

Diced-up black bananas in sauerkraut fondue!

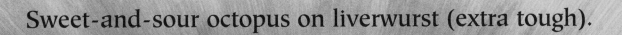

Sweet-and-sour octopus on liverwurst (extra tough).

OK, I think that's plenty!

ENOUGH,

ENOUGH,

ENOUGH!

Shhhhh, I think she's coming.

HIDE
OVER
THERE!

Hey, I can still see your messy monster hair!

Oh yeah? I can see your big round googly eyes and your
giant monster ears and your...

SQUEAK

SURPRISE!!!!